Flower Fairy Tales
of the
Language of Flowers

Volume II

THE STORY

OF

TWO SHEPHERDESSES,

THE BLONDE AND THE BRUNETTE :

AND OF A

QUEEN OF FRANCE.

---

by Taxile Delord, translated by N. Cleveland,
edited by m stewart, illustrated by J.J. Grandville

earthly pursuits (www.earthlypursuits.com)
2010

Also available:

Flower Fairy Tales of the Language of Flowers - Volume 1

(The Flower Fairy, The Poet Jacobus and The Pansy and
lists of flower names in English, French and Latin
with their meanings.)

Table of Contents

THE FLOWER FAIRY

One fine spring evening, as the Flower Fairy was gently rocking in her hammock of interwoven convolvuli, idly thinking of those other mysterious flowers, which we call stars, suddenly she thought she heard a distant rustling—a confused noise. "It is the sylphs," thought she, "who come to woo the flowers;" and she relapsed into her revery. But soon the sounds become louder, and the gold sand resounded under steps more and more distinct. The fairy sat erect, and beheld approaching a long procession of flowers. They were of all ages, and of every rank. Full-blown Roses, already on their decline, there walked, surrounded by their young families of buds. All distinctions were overlooked. The aristocratic Tulip gave her arm to the vulgar and plebeian Pink. The Geranium, proud as a financier, walked side by side with the tender Anemone—and the haughty Amaryllis listened without much disdain, to the rather vulgar conversation of the Bladder-nut-tree. As often happens in well arranged societies, at times of great emergency, a forced reconciliation had taken place among the flowers.

Lilies, with their brows encircled by fireflies and the Bellflowers, with glow-worms shining like living lanterns among their petals lighted the procession, which was brought up, in a somewhat disorderly manner, by a careless troop of Daisies.

The procession drew up in good order before the palace of the astonished fairy, and an eloquent Hellebore, stepping from the ranks, thus addressed her:—

"Your Majesty:

"The flowers here present beg you to accept their homage, and to lend a favorable ear to their humble complaint. For thousands of years we have supplied mankind with their themes of comparison; we alone have given them all their metaphors; indeed, without us poetry could not exist. Men lend to us their virtues and their vices; their good and their bad qualities;—and it is time that we should have some experience of what these are. We are tired of the flower-life. We wish for permission to assume the human form, and to judge, for ourselves, whether that which they say above, of our character, is agreeable to truth."

...we must inform you that the fairy did not grant the desired permission without silently resolving that she would be revenged.

The next morning her garden was a desert...

[For the complete story of The Flower Fairy, see Volume 1 of *Flower Fairy Tales of the Language of Flowers.*]

Lis

Lily

Lilium

Bleuet and Coquelicot

Annual Bluebottle and Corn poppy

Centaurea cyanus and Papaver rhœas

THE STORY

OF

TWO SHEPHERDESSES,

THE BLONDE AND THE BRUNETTE,

AND OF A

QUEEN OF FRANCE.

I.

The prettiest girls in the village, beyond all dispute, are Bleuette and Coquelicot;—Bleuette, with her fair hair and blue eyes;—Coquelicot, with form so elastic, and her bright rosy cheeks.

"Faith!" said the country judge, a few days since, "Bleuette looks charmingly, when, with modest air and downcast eyes, she trips over the village green."

"Udsbuddikins!" exclaimed the village squire, last Sunday, while seeing his vassals dance,—"this little Coquelicot has a most enchanting way of dancing. I am certain that there is not, at court, a more graceful girl. See, there, what vassals I have."

In fact, it would have been impossible to find two prettier faces than those of Coquelicot and Bleuette. They dwelt in the same cottage—sung the same songs—tended the same turtle-doves—and they had but one flock between them.

The only thing not held by them in common, was their hearts. Bleuette had promised hers to Lucas, while Coquelicot had sworn eternal affection for Blaise.

In every other respect they were very prudent.

Notwithstanding that good fortune so often provokes envy, everybody in the village loved Bleuette and Coquelicot. If the wolf strangled a sheep or two in the neighborhood, he never meddled with the flock of Bleuette and Coquelicot. If master Renard mercilessly twisted the necks of Maturin's, of Bruneau's, or of Thibaut's fowls, he always respected those of Coquelicot and Bleuette.

The hail-storm never harmed the raspberries on their bushes, nor the grapes on their trellis. Their hives were always filled with the richest honey. They were happy,—and so happy, that many persons, and especially the schoolmaster, maintained that they were fairies, or at least the fairies' god-daughters.

It is well known, that whenever they seated themselves under a tree, a nightingale would immediately alight thereon; or if they walked, arm in arm, through the paths in the wheat field, the cricket and the grasshopper would advance to the edge of the furrow, to salute them on their way, and sing their welcome,—as well becomes a polite grasshopper, and a cricket who knows his duty.

II.
WHAT THE TWO SHEPHERDESSES SAY TO ONE ANOTHER
BEFORE THEY GO TO BED.

"Another happy day, dear Bleuette, has glided away."

"To be succeeded, dear Coquelicot, by one like it on the morrow."

"Dost thou regret thy old form?"

"Wouldst *thou* cease to be a woman?"

"No."

"Neither would I."

"How fortunate that we selected this modest village, where we can live so quietly. Happiness is found only in the country."

"With Lucas, who is so good."

"And with Blaise, who plays the bagpipe so well."

"Nothing in the world is so delightful as to be a woman."

"To be happy, one must have a heart."

Then the two maidens placed themselves before their mirror.

"Am I not prettier than when I was only a bluebottle?" said one.

"Who would not prefer me to all the corn-poppies on earth?" added the other.

Thus the blonde and the brunette would converse together every evening. Then they would embrace each other, and sleep until the first cooings of their turtles awoke them.

III.

A COUNTRY JUDGE'S IDEA.

Finding himself worn out, wrinkled and withered, the country judge began to think of marrying; and inasmuch as he was humpbacked, lame, toothless, bald, and asthmatic, he concluded that he ought to have the prettiest girl in the village. And thus it was that he cast his eyes on Bleuette.

IV.

A SQUIRE'S NOTION.

The squire of the village lived in an old, cracked tower, which admitted rain, wind, hail, snow, and was open, indeed, to all kinds of weather. His only domestic was a peasant, who attended to the hogs by day, and at evening waited on his master. But this did not hinder him from talking of his chateau, and of his servants. He possessed, nevertheless, the right of jurisdiction, both high and low, over a territory which no longer belonged to him, and through the space of a league around, could hang any one he pleased.

One fine day, when his gout, his catarrh, and his rheumatism left him a little ease, it occurred to him, that hitherto he had been living a selfish life;—and, noble gentleman as he was, he formed the generous resolution to share, henceforth, with some human being, the advantages of his position; he determined, in fact, to insure the happiness of some woman. His choice rested on Coquelicot.

V.

THE TWO DELICATE-COLORED TUNICS.

In the mean time, the two shepherdesses, unsuspicious of the honors which were about to descend upon them, were quietly enjoying the love of their shepherds.

Lucas sung his woes in a silken tunic of palest green, while Blaise, in a coat of blue not less delicate than his friend's green one, made all the region round echo to the strains of his rural pipes. The fleece of Robin, Bleuette's favorite sheep, was not more curly than the hair of Lucas. The cheeks of Blaise were so plump and round, that he always looked as if blowing a pipe. When they were seen together, in their coats of pale blue and green, with their crooks and shepherd-bags, ornamented with ribands, everybody declared that shepherds so perfect as Lucas and Blaise, could not help loving shepherdesses so accomplished as Bleuette and Coquelicot.

Bleuette and Coquelicot had promised their lovers, to pay them with a kiss for the first nest of nightingales which they should bring to them. To do this, they would have to wait only a year; so that Lucas and Blaise were the happiest of mortals.

VI.

A PHILOSOPHICAL REFLECTION.

Human happiness is transient as a shadow!

VII.

REGRETS.

As Lucas and Blaise were walking over the fields, thinking of the felicity which awaited them at the end of the year, they met Bleuette and Coquelicot, who were weeping bitterly.

The shepherds began to weep also, without well knowing why. Lucas first saw the propriety of asking for an explanation.

"That prettiest of sheep—Robin—is he sick, my dear shepherdess?" asked he, in a voice soft as the hue of his tunic.

"Has my Coquelicot lost the turtle-dove which I gave her last spring?" said Blaise.

"Robin is very well," replied Bleuette; "but I have seen the Judge, who said to me—'Pretty one, I mean to marry thee.'"

"And I," said Coquelicot, "have seen the squire, who said to me—'Lass, thou shalt be my wife.'"

The two shepherds immediately made lamentable moans. Blaise swore that he would throw himself down a precipice. Lucas wished to hang himself with the string of his shepherd's scrip—a string which Bleuette had given him.

Here was a scene to soften Hyrcanian tigers.

"And, worst of all," added the two shepherdesses, "the squire and the judge are coming for us this evening and if we refuse to go, they will send the soldiers, and compel us to accompany them."

The shepherds declared that they would die sooner than lose the objects of their love,—and all four then set out for the village.

The cottage of Bleuette and Coquelicot was already beset by the soldiers. The squire and the judge came towards their betrothed. When these were about to resist, the archers at once surrounded them. Too sensitive to endure so cruel a sight, Blaise and Lucas fainted away.

"Alas!" exclaimed Bleuette and Coquelicot, as they were hurried off, "we were too much elated with our felicity. It were better to have remained humble flowers, lost in the furrows. We had not then been compelled to marry a squire who has the gout, or a humpbacked judge. Farewell, Lucas! Farewell, Blaise! Farewell forever! We have none to protect us—none to rescue us."

As they were indulging in these lamentations, a throng of villagers came in sight upon the road. These good people had their hands full of green branches, and were singing in chorus—

"Oh, blissful day!—of hope the spring!

Our queen returns;—sing, peasants, sing;—

Her welcome shout!"—

The rest of this chorus, which was full of poetry, and well adapted to the place, was drowned in loud and oft-repeated cries of "Long live the Flower de Luce!"—"Long live the Queen of France!" The queen had just arrived.

The squire, taken by surprise, was unable to present to her, on a plate of gold, the keys of his chateau—and this annoyed him beyond description. The judge, equally unprepared, found it out of his power to make an address to the queen—a disappointment which might have made him sick, had it not been the day appointed for his marriage.

VIII.

THE FLOWER DE LUCE,
QUEEN OF FRANCE.

At the sight of the queen, hope revived in the hearts of Bleuette and Coquelicot.

Like them, the queen was young and beautiful. Her tall, elastic form,—her pallid countenance,—and the extreme mildness of her eyes, impressed all who beheld her, as with some secret, powerful charm. One no sooner saw her, than he felt himself attracted towards her.

The two shepherdesses threw themselves at her feet, kissed the edge of her long white robe, and wept.

The queen gently raised them, and inquired into the cause of their grief.

"The village squire would force me to marry him"

"I am compelled to become the wife of the judge,"—together replied Coquelicot and Bleuette.

The queen, with a smile, turned her eyes from the two young girls, to the two old men. This short survey was enough.

"Follow me," said she to the suppliants; "we will look into the matter. It shall never be said that the Queen of France sees tears shed by her subjects, without attempting to dry them."

The royal train immediately resumed its march, and the peasants followed, making the air resound with their acclamations. They sung many other choruses suited to the occasion—such as you may easily find in any of the comic operas.

Flower de Luce had in the neighborhood a country residence, to which she came every summer, that she might forget there the cares of greatness and a throne. Thither she conducted the two shepherdesses. Before retiring to her own apartments, she summoned before her the squire and the judge. Instead of giving them the harsh reception which they deserved, she administered a gentle rebuke, friendly rather than severe. She showed them the danger of ill-matched unions,—she made them feel how wrong it is to employ force in matters of love,—and having finished her remarks, gave them permission, since they were so bent on marriage, to espouse, each of them, one of her ladies of honor, whom she endowed handsomely. The younger of these ladies had passed her fiftieth year.

This over, she directed that she should be left alone with the two shepherdesses.

When these three again found themselves together, the queen removed her diadem, as well as a shield of golden flower de luces, which was attached to her robe—but an air of majesty still sat upon her brow, and the two shepherdesses continued to regard her—as we are apt to do the great ones of earth—trembling and with downcast eyes.

Flower de Luce seemed to feel a momentary pleasure in witnessing this embarrassment. She was, however, the first to speak.

"How is this, dear sisters;—do you not recognize me?"

At these words, Bleuette and Coquelicot raised their eyes. A secret foreboding—a sudden flash of thought, crossed their minds at the same instant.

"The Lily!" they both exclaimed.

"The same," replied the queen. "I at once discovered, under the costume of the shepherdesses, my old companions, Bleuette and Coquelicot. The flowers owe each other mutual aid on earth; and I am glad that I came in season to save you from the bold schemes of this old squire and this miserable judge."

The three flowers then proceeded to speak of all which had happened to them since they had left the garden of the fairy. Bleuette and Coquelicot dwelt long on the happiness of being beloved by such shepherds as Blaise and Lucas.

"Beloved," murmured the Lily,— "oh yes, it must be delightful."

Bleuette and Coquelicot did not understand this reflection. They thought of nothing but complimenting the Lily on the brilliant position and high rank which she held in the world.

"Be in no haste to congratulate me," replied the Lily: "listen first to my story."

"Many years ago I lived on the border of a lonely lake, in a small castle which was hidden among the trees. Every morning I rose with the dawn, and hailed the rising sun. At evening, I watched his decline, and his departure seemed to take away my life. As if they had been the only source of my strength, each ray, as it disappeared, left me more inclined to the earth. But the sparkling stars again restored my powers. I loved, at evening, to sit upon my terrace, and feel the pearl-drops of dew, as they stood upon my brow, and quivered in my hair. Sometimes, when the heat was oppressive, I used to lean over the water, and inhale the freshness of the wave, which gave me back my image.

"My only companion was an Ermine, which had found a refuge in this remote solitude. Each evening and morning she came to wash, in the lake, her delicate, white fur. The Ermine, at our first interview, assured me that she felt drawn towards me by some secret sympathy. We seemed influenced by the same love of solitude—the same dread of vulgar contact—the same modest reserve.

"Without knowing exactly why, I also loved the Ermine.

"Thus might I have continued to live happy,— thanks to the sun, the stars, the dew, the cool air and water of the lake,—and I should add, thanks to my wise friend, the Ermine. But one day a traveller, who had lost his way, knocked at the door of my castle. I could not refuse him its hospitality while the storm raged without.

"The stranger was in a hunting-dress. He was young, and his aspect was frank and noble. He told me that in the heat of the chase, he had got separated from his companions, and being prevented by the storm from retracing his steps, he had ventured to knock at the door of my castle, little expecting, added he, to find so fair a hostess.

"This speech made me blush.

"Having prepared his repast, and whatever else his situation required, I was about to retire.

"'Your pardon,' said the stranger, in a voice gentle but thrilling—'if you flee from me, I shall believe that, deceived by some sweet though cruel illusion, I have but dreamed that a fairy appeared to me. If thou art a woman, stay!'

"In spite of myself, I did stay.

"We were just sitting down to table, when a loud clatter of horses, with horns and trumpets, was heard at the castle-gate. It was the retinue of my guest. They had discovered his track, and had come to find him This unknown stranger, dear sisters, was the king of France.

"On taking his leave of me, he bent his knee, seized and kissed my hand, and in a low voice, said,—'Noblest and fairest of the fair, I must now leave thee,—but I shall return.'

"Full well he kept his promise.

"I told my friend the Ermine, of the king's attentions, and of the offer which he had made me of his hand.

"'Remember,' said she, 'that true greatness and genuine purity can live only in solitude. Take pattern from the lily, my child. We acknowledge its beauty, chiefly because that to its beauty, it joins an air of guileless innocence, which charms the heart.'

"This allusion troubled me. Alas! thought I, she does not know how much haughtier the Lily became, on the day when she requested that she might no longer be a flower. I promised, nevertheless, that I would obey the Ermine's advice.

"But the king, in urging his suit, showed a pertinacity so refined, and a passion so ardent, that I at last consented to be his. I was no longer a flower—I was a woman. My weakness was the weakness of my sex.

"The king told me how much good I could do when on the throne, and how delightful it would be thus to make myself beloved. I was bound too, he added, to bless him and his race. I consented to be crowned.

"Henceforth, adieu to the sun, the stars, the pearly dew-drops, and the lake. Now etiquette controls and besets me, and I sigh amid crowds of courtiers. My old friend, the Ermine, to whom I gave free admission to the palace, comes there no more, through fear of being sullied. A few nights since, I had a frightful dream. I beheld the lilies all draggled in the dirt, and a beautiful young queen, whom they were leading to the scaffold!

"How much I regret the time when, yet a simple flower, I was the cherished symbol of innocence! Then was I strown in the path of virgins and chaste brides. Angel messengers from heaven would stop a while to repose among my petals, and on the morrow, taking me along in their arms, would present me to men, as a fresh pledge of the good tidings which they came to announce. Then I lived on air, on light and sunshine. My nights were passed in looking at the stars, and in the intoxicating delights of those confused murmurs which one hears in the shade:—whilst now"—

The queen burst into tears.

Bleuette and Coquelicot endeavored to console her. They told her that she should not magnify her troubles,—that every situation had more or less of discomfort, and that her misfortunes had arisen from selecting a position too elevated. They then adduced their own example. If, instead of being a queen, you had, like us, been only a simple villager, would you ever have deplored your lot? Ever since you were a Lily, sister, you have been a little too much given to pride. This vice has done you great harm. You must trust it no longer, but practise patience.

After these just remarks, Coquelicot and Bleuette asked the queen's permission to depart, that they might go and relieve the anxiety of Blaise and Lucas. The permission was granted,—and with it, the queen gave two large diamonds for themselves, and for Blaise and Lucas, two bunches of trinkets.

IX.

THE RETURN.

As they crossed the palace-court, the courtiers, who were assembled there in great numbers, could not help exclaiming,—"Zounds! There are two pretty girls!"

Coquelicot and Bleuette did not even look round, at this compliment, in such haste were they again to see Lucas and Blaise.

After walking a little way, they began to run. Away they go, leaping over the high tops of the lucerne—treading under foot the clover—startling the lark upon his nest in the furrow, and the frog that was asleep on the bank of the stream. Away, away they go—hardly taking breath—walking and running alternately.

In this way they reached the village before night.

They hastened towards their cottage, expecting to find Blaise and Lucas on the threshold—resolved, in their despair, that they would die on the spot that was so dear to them.

They met two bridal processions.

One was that of Lucas, who married Margot, the daughter of Big-Peter, and the other that of Blaise, who espoused Flipotte, the niece of Big-John.

The ingrates still wore in their hats the ribands which they had received from Coquelicot and Bleuette.

As soon as they saw the pale blue and the pale green tunic in the arms of their rivals, Bleuette and Coquelicot seemed as though smitten by a thunderbolt. They fell, never to rise again. Lucas and Blaise lost, that day, two fond hearts, and two bunches of handsome trinkets.

X.

IT IS ALL OVER.

In the village grave-yard a modest tomb has been erected for Bleuette and Coquelicot. Thither, from all the country round, lovers come yearly, on a sort of pilgrimage.

About this tomb bluebottles and cornpoppies grow in abundance. Nowhere else are their hues so bright and delicate. You would say that the flowers have caught something from the character of those two shepherdesses.

History will long seek in vain for an instance of devoted affection equal to theirs.

The grasshopper and the cricket have taken up their abode in the high grass, which grows about the grave of Bleuette and Coquelicot. Day and night they chant around it their mournful ditties.

A nightingale likewise comes before sunrise, and, concealed in the branches of a willow near, sings her farewell to the two shepherdesses.

The butterflies and the bees are lonely, as they flit round among the neighboring flowers. The reckless gad-fly and the humming-fly dare not disturb, with their noisy wings, the stillness of this mausoleum.

Often, as the schoolmaster passes through the cemetery, he stops to cull flowers from the tomb of the two victims. "My dear children," he says to his pupils, while he shows them the bluebottle and the cornpoppy,—"this one signifies delicacy, and the other, consolation." These are two qualities, that have no very direct connection with the story which we relate to you. But we must give up in the presence of the master. He knows better than we do the language of flowers. And yet the young folks of the village take a pleasure, when they have a chance, in twitching his queue, and playing other pranks upon him.

In order to excuse themselves in the eyes of posterity, for having caused the death of two shepherdesses so delightful as Bleuette and Coquelicot, Lucas and Blaise solemnly affirmed, upon their death-beds, their belief at the time, that the marriage with the judge and the squire had actually been consummated.

Fifty years after the death of their victims, Lucas and Blaise die, overwhelmed with remorse.

The following is the inscription on their tomb:—

HERE REPOSE

BLAISE and LUCAS;

They were

Good fathers, good husbands, good shepherds.

Whosoever thou art,

Stay a moment: drop a tear to their

memories;

Say a prayer for their souls.

R. I. P.

THE FLOWER OF OUR CHOICE.

They who love flowers, have always one which enjoys the preference.

This is the flower of remembrance,—the flower of love,—the flower of youth. It is the flower which we gather in the first days of life's spring.

We associate the name and the features of the woman we love, with the thought of that flower, which never fails to remind us of her.

With some, this flower is the rose, the jessamine, the lilac, the heliotrope, or the vervain. Others prefer the periwinkle, the violet, or the pansy. In each case, the remembrance of some woman is inseparable from that of the flower.

The perfume of one's favorite flower causes a sort of intoxication, which affects the heart, without disturbing the head.

The sight of it calls you away from the present, and you live once more in the past. It brings before you that narrow path, where together you used to walk, grazing the bushes laden with dew, and that stream in which you often saw her image. You hear again her voice—the gentle voice; it seems to address you.

At another time you say to yourself, this is the flower which my mother loved, or this is the one which my sister wore.

And then you think of your childhood; of that mother who still looks down upon you from above, and that sister, who was so chaste, pure, and beautiful, that God took her to be one of his angels.

Unhappy the man who has never had his eyes fill with tears at the sight of a particular flower.

Such a one can have been neither a child nor a youth. He can have had neither mother, sister, nor affianced bride. He never loved.

This is the flower which we wear at our button-hole—which we place by our pillow,—or send in bouquets to our best friends.

The favorite flower brings good luck.

One should have his flower upon earth, as he has his star in the skies.

Trust none who deride this as superstition.

My chosen flower is the jessamine.

While this is in bloom, a lively, pleasing, thrilling sensation seems to pervade my soul;—a sort of enjoyment which departs when the jessamine begins to fade.

Between me and the jessamine there exists an intimate union. True, it recalls to my mind things innumerable;—but it is not my story that I am going to tell you. Indeed, you already know it—for it is the same as your own.

Flower of our choice!—sweet, delightful flower—whose name we gently whisper, as we do that of the woman we love—the heart which no longer confesses thy mysterious charm, is a heart forever withered.

It may beat still, but it no longer palpitates; it may live, but it has ceased to feel.

Long keep for me thy perfume—keep it ever,—and on my tombstone let these words appear:—"One only love—one only flower."

THE FLOWER OF HOME.

Every country has its particular flower. In Brittany it is the Broom; in Auvergne, the Lavender; in Normandy, the star-like Apple-blossom. The valleys of Touraine abound in Lilies; the meads of Languedoc are enamelled with the finest Daisies; while in Berry the banks of the streams are adorned with fresh Lilies of the Valley.

Do you know the Cassia? It is the flower of Provence—the flower of my native country.

Its leaf is scolloped like lace. It grows on a prickly bush, which blooms in autumn. When the roses have all faded,—when the flowers of the honeysuckle have disappeared,—and when the inodorous pomegranate is displaying its bright tufts, the cassia diffuses far and wide its fragrance.

Its stem is so short that it cannot be made into bouquets. The young maidens hold it between their rosy lips, on which it glows like a little ball of gold.

When the exile beholds the flower of his home, he longs to return; and while inhaling its perfume, he fancies, for a moment, that he feels the breezes of his native clime.

I have seen lilies blooming on the banks of foreign streams. As the wind bent down their tall stems, I almost fancied that they were inclining their heads to welcome a compatriot and friend.

Poor lilies! I found them all drooping, with their pale cups moistened by tears. You would have thought that they were sighing, as well as I, at the thought of France.

As one weeps when he hears again the clocks of his native town, or the strains of some melody which he used to sing in his boyhood, so the sight of the home-flower will often start a tear.

It looks at you—it recognizes you—it speaks to you:—

"I am thy sister: place me again on the hill—in the valley—in the midst of the meadows—on the bank of the stream, where I was born.

"There the breeze is more gentle, the waters are cooler, the groves have a softer murmur, and the songs of birds are more melodious.

"Far from my country, I languish here. Take me back! Take me back!"

Thus speaks the flower of our own land.

Happy those who find it on their way. It is the soothing voice of memory, which speaks to them from its fragrant corolla.

The golden broom, the blue-eared lavender, the drooping lily, white daisies, and lilies of the valley, fresh and sweet-scented, grow in many places. But there is one flower which is found only in Provence—that flower is the cassia, the flower of my home.

NOCTURNE.
NIGHT-FLOWERS.

———————————————

I LOVE you, flowers of night! I prefer you to all your sisters that look so brilliant by day.

When the sun has sunk below the horizon, and the shadows, like long, drooping eyelashes, fall from the branches, then the flower of night unfolds, and the first beams of the evening star come and sport in its corolla.

The flowers and the stars are sisters. What do they say to one another?

They talk of the ennui which they feel during the day; they interchange rays and perfume; they mingle their soul with the mighty soul of nature.

Does some hair-brained sylph come to interfere with their discourse? The night-flower pays no heed—she is no coquette.

She loves only those who suffer.

Like the sound of the wind—like the murmuring of waters—the fragrance of the night-flower is consoling.

She listens to the complaint of the shepherd; she smiles at the reveries of the young girl; she lends an ear to the poet's song.

Her delicate perfume gives a secret charm to your first tender meeting—spreading over you, as it were, a veil of innocence and of purity.

No insect alights upon the flower of night. The phalæna hums around it; it may even touch its calyx—but it dares not stay there.

Sometimes, however, a fairy will plunge into the recesses of its petals, to escape from some persecuting goblin.

From her palace, the marvel of Peru, the fair Titania proceeds every night to make excursions through her nocturnal empire.

There is an hour when woods rustle—when waters murmur—when lovers talk—when poets sing—when confused sounds and soft sighs fill all the plain; it is then that the night-flower is most expanded.

Rustlings, murmurs, sighs, and echoes—poets' songs and amorous breathings—all mingle in the air, and descend upon nature in the dew.

With her portion of this gentle rain is formed, in the depths of the night-flower, a bright liquid pearl. This pearl shakes and quivers there. The slightest breath of air can break it—and the morning wind will soon rise.

To preserve this precious pearl, formed during the night, the nocturnal flower closes its petals by day.

Thus, too, the poet shuts carefully in his heart those treasures of thought which he has gathered in his solitude.

It is for such reasons that I love the night-blooming flower, and prefer her to her sisters, which are so brilliant by day.

AUBADE.
THE EARLIEST FLOWER.

It is morning: rise, young girls,—let us go and gather the first flower—the May-flower.

Place it in your bosom, and preserve it carefully; it brings good fortune all the rest of the year.

I shall give to thee, Madeleine, the one which I pluck, and thou wilt place it among thy tresses.

The first flower is not the primrose, nor the periwinkle, nor the hyacinth, nor the violet, nor the lily of the valley.

It is not that which blooms first in the succession of the seasons. It is the flower which first meets your eye—which you come upon by accident.

Last year it was the violet which announced to me the return of spring; this year, it was the rose. Who can tell me what flower will mark for me the spring which is next to come?

What does it matter?

Whatever thou mayest be, first flower, everybody loves thee, and receives thee with delight. Who can see thee, and not feel his eye grow moist?

While we look at thee, the youth of our heart seems about to be renewed with the youth of the year; our spirit is ready to bloom with the corolla of the flower, and our feelings grow green again with its leaves.

First flower, which we meet when we go out on May-day morning,—thou art *hope*—thou are *illusion*. Thou makest us believe it possible that the past may return.

When, on certain days and at certain hours, we meet with some object of ancient worship, the mind goes back to antiquity; it leaps, in an instant, over the mighty interval, and fancies that it has reconstructed the chain of time.

For a moment we seem about to enter on a new career. But soon the soul, exhausted by fatigue, returns to its starting-point, and remains motionless.

And thus, too, the sight of the first flower revives within us a host of buried thoughts. They awake—they spread their white pinions—they fly gayly round. We fancy that they are about to conduct us far, very far towards the home of our youth.

Alas! The first spring-flower has but just withered, and our fancies have already slackened their flight; they fall to the ground, and their frail wings are shattered.

Blessings on thee, nevertheless, blessings, thou first flower, for this short, intoxicating hour of thy gift. For a moment to believe that one is again young—that he loves, and is happy—is not this to live whole years?

It is morn: rise, young girls,—let us go and gather the first flower—the May-flower.

Place it in your bosom—keep it with care. It brings good fortune for the rest of the year.

Here, Madeleine, is the flower which I have plucked. Inhale its fragrance, and then place it among thy tresses.

A PETITION.
THE FLOWERS OF THE BALL-ROOM.

We are the flowers of the ball-room—the unhappy victims of gay festivities.

Timid and reserved, we come with no adornment but our own simple charms; and we have to contend with those flowers of the mine called diamonds.

Those children of fire, the opal, the amethyst, the turquoise, and the topaz, sparkle in the lamp-light.

But we, who are daughters of the air and the dew,—we open our eyes to look only at the moon and the stars. The atmosphere of the dance dries and consumes us. Within a quarter of an hour we wither.

Why, young maiden, dost thou place us among thy beautiful tresses? Look on thy toilet-table. Hast thou not flowers there, made by human hands? – flowers which fear not the heat, nor the dust, nor the light of lustres, nor the jostling of the crowd? Take us not, young lady, to the ball. Leave us to bathe our pliant feet in these crystal vases. We will perfume thy apartment; and when thou shalt return, pale, weary, and pensive, we will greet thee with smiles, and will mingle sweet dreams with thy sleep.

O! take us not, young lady, to the ball.

Alas! she heeds not. We are twined in a fresh garland for her hair; we are blooming upon her bosom. Come, then; we must needs go. We are the flowers of the ball-room—the unhappy victims of gay festivities.

One by one, our petals will be pulled out, and will be trodden under foot. Ere the ball is over, we shall lose our place in these tresses—this cincture will hold us no longer. To-morrow some coarse servant will pick us up and throw us into the street.

Once more, young maiden, we entreat thee, leave us here, in thy virgin chamber, where we are so happy.

Thou art going.—Take care, young woman! living flower of society,—sprightly ornament of the ball,—lest, treating thee as it treats us, the world shall one day tread thee under foot, and leave thee in the street.

ELEGIE.
THE WOUNDED FLOWER.

The morning dews made me blow, and I expanded just as the sun rose.

Now I am about to die.

A young girl was passing me this morning, and stopped to look at me. She seemed to me so handsome, that I smiled upon her.

While she passed caressingly her hand over my leaves, a thrill of joy ran through me. But, in a moment after, an acute pain struck me to the heart and, half broken, I hung down on my stem.

Why, young maiden, didst thou not pluck me off at once? Then, instead of this long agony, I should have been resting, at peace, in thy virgin bosom.

The blood oozes from my wound; a mortal coldness blanches my leaves; my corolla is closing; scarcely can I now hear the sweet murmur of the breeze among the leaves. The birds no longer sing; the sun has disappeared from my view. Sisters, dear sisters, is it night already?

No: it is death which is spreading over me its shade. No more shall I behold the sparkling stars; no more spread open my corolla, a perfumed casket, to receive the diamonds of the dew. My mortal remains will soon strew the ground; and my soul, ascending to heaven, will leave behind it only its fragrant trail.

My ghost, young girl, will appear to thee. It will reproach thee for thy carelessness and cruelty. Remorse will become my avenger. But

no; I forgive thee. Mayest thou, on thy part never
feel what I, a wounded flower, endure!

visit www.earthlypursuits.com
for more of *The Flowers Personified*

Bleuette & Coquelicot

meaning: Delicacy & Ephemeral charms

hand-colored illustration
engraved on steel by J.N. Gimbrede
from designs by J.J. Grandville for *Les Fleurs Animees*

introduction by Alphonse Kerr
text by Taxile Delord
translated by N. Cleaveland
published by M. Martin in New York as
The Flowers Personified—1847

The Lily

meaning: Majesty

hand-colored illustration
engraved on steel by J.N. Gimbrede
from designs by J.J. Grandville for *Les Fleurs Animees*

introduction by Alphonse Kerr
text byTaxile Delord
translated by N. Cleaveland
published by M. Martin in New York as
The Flowers Personified—1847

www.ingramcontent.com/pod-product-compliance
Lightning Source LLC
Chambersburg PA
CBHW071216130626
46555CB00004B/1731